The Little Cat Baby

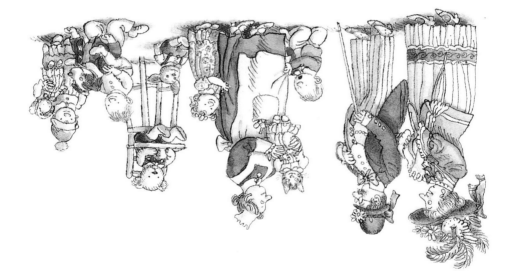

ALLAN AHLBERG

The Little Cat Baby

Illustrated by Fritz Wegner

DIAL BOOKS FOR YOUNG READERS  NEW YORK

First published in the United States 2004 by
Dial Books for Young Readers
A division of Penguin Young Readers Group
345 Hudson Street
New York, New York 10014
Published in Great Britain 2003 by Puffin Books

Text copyright © 2003 by Allan Ahlberg
Illustrations copyright © 2003 by Fritz Wegner

Text set in Goudy Old Style
Printed in Italy

1 3 5 7 9 10 8 6 4 2

Library of Congress Cataloging-in-Publication Data
Ahlberg, Allan.
The little cat baby / by Allan Ahlberg ; pictures by Fritz Wegner.
p. cm.
Summary: A man and woman go to Nurse Doodle's Baby
Shop and find a little cat baby to be their very own.
ISBN 0-8037-3012-8
[1. Cats—Fiction. 2. Babies—Fiction.] I. Wegner, Fritz, ill. II. Title.
PZ7.A2688 Li 2004
[E]—dc22
2003055740

Nurse Doodle's Shop

Once upon a topsy-turvy time
in the middle of a long hot winter
there was a woman and a man who wanted a baby.
So off they went to the Baby Shop,
which was how it was done in those days.

Nurse Doodle showed them lots of babies.

There was a pink baby

and a brown baby

and a green baby

and a flowerpot-throwing baby

and a robot baby–
all in pieces in a box–

and a crybaby

and a bouncing baby

and . . .

a little cat baby.

"Oh, my!" said the woman and the man together.
"Look at that little cat baby!"

So then the woman and the man
picked out the little cat baby,
and Nurse Doodle wrapped her up in a nice new blanket.

The woman and the man also chose
a cat-baby basket,
a cat-baby bottle,
and a book of cat-baby bedtime stories.

Then they went home.

More Milk

The topsy-turvy times continued.
Soon the little cat baby
learned to lap her milk up from a saucer
and wash her face and whiskers with her paw.
After a week or so she learned to talk.

The first word that she ever spoke, of course,
was "Meow!"
the second, "Purr!"
and the third and fourth, "More milk."
"Oh, my!" said the woman and the man together.
"Listen to that little cat baby!"

The woman and the man just loved their little cat baby.
They stroked her baby fur till it shone.
They bought her a red flea collar
with a bell on it.
Also, as she got older,
they put a cat flap in the kitchen door...

just for her.

The Harum-Scarum Night

One night–
it was a harum-scarum night,
full of huge shadows
and fireworks going off–
the little cat baby woke up.

Down the stairs she went, across the hall
and out through the cat flap.

The little cat baby sat on the wall.
Nearby, some men were playing tennis by flashlight,
which was how it was done in those . . . nights.
Also, in the next-door neighbor's garden,
a little dog baby was burying a bone.

All of a sudden, a huge shadow,
like a giant feathery hand–
though it was only some branches, really–
fell on the wall.
It made that little cat baby jump
almost out of her furry skin.

Off she ran,
down the trafficky street,

across the fireworky park,
under the spooky bridge,

full of more shadows
and pairs of eyes,
up somebody else's garden path . . .

and through *their* cat flap.

The Strange House

There were strange noises in the strange house:
crashing noises,
clanking noises,
wailing noises.

A light was shining through a doorway.
The little cat baby–
curious as a cat, of course–
peeked in.

And saw . . .

Nurse Doodle!
(It was *her* house. The shop was in the front.)

All Nurse Doodle's shopful of babies
were awake that night,
even the robot baby,
whose pieces had been put together,
not to mention the flowerpot-throwing baby,
who was . . .

throwing flowerpots.

When morning came–
it was a helter-skelter morning, full of parades–
Nurse Doodle took the little cat baby home.

"Oh, my!" said the woman and the man together.
"Here comes our little cat baby!"
And they grabbed her up and stroked her baby fur...

till it shone.

The Christmas Ladder

And still the topsy-turvy times continued.
In the sunny month of December,
the little cat baby won second prize in the baby show,
and first prize . . .

in the cat show!

The following evening, which was *Christmas* Eve,
the woman and the man
took their little prize-winning baby to the park.

The little cat baby swung on the swings,
fed the ducks, *chased* the ducks,
had a moonlight picnic with her mom and dad–
and climbed the Christmas Ladder.

Her presents, she knew, were waiting at the top.
After all,
that was how it was *always* done...

"...IN THOSE DAYS

The End